CHARLIE BROWN'S ALL-STARS

BY CHARLES M. SCHULZ

WORLD PUBLISHING
TIMES MIRROR
NEW YORK

Published by The World Publishing Company
110 East 59th Street, New York City, New York 10022
Published simultaneously in Canada
by Nelson, Foster & Scott Ltd.

1972 Printing

Illustrations from the Bill Melendez–Lee Mendelson
television production "It's the Great Pumpkin, Charlie Brown!"

Library of Congress Catalog Card Number: 66-21127
ISBN: 0-529-04875-2

Printed in the United States of America

WORLD PUBLISHING
TIMES MIRROR

TO GEORGE, WITH FRIENDSHIP

To look at Charlie Brown, you wouldn't think he was a baseball fanatic.

But, then again, maybe you would.

He always walked around with an oversize cap on his head, and a glove that was at least big enough to catch a small pumpkin.

Charlie Brown's life was an especially difficult one because he was both manager and pitcher, and the way he filled these roles left him open to lots of criticism from the players on his team.

"HEY, MANAGER!" Frieda complained. "Why do I have to play way out there in the outfield? Nobody can see my naturally curly hair!"

"WATCH WHERE YOU'RE THROWING THAT BALL, CHARLIE BROWN!" said Lucy. "That last pitch of yours flew clear over the backstop and almost hit my mother!"

The game that day didn't go very well.

In fact, Charlie Brown's team lost by a score of 123 to 0, and
to make matters worse, Charlie Brown himself dropped a fly ball
in the last inning that he really should have caught.

"THIS TEAM WILL NEVER AMOUNT TO ANYTHING!" screamed Lucy in disgust. "I refuse to play center field for a sinking ship!"

"I'm sorry
Charlie Brown,"
said Shermy.
"But I guess
I'll quit too.
It's depressing
to play for a team
that always loses.
I'm the sort
who needs to win
once in a while.
It's different with you.
I think you get sort of
a neurotic pleasure
out of losing all the time!"

Poor Charlie Brown.
Even his dog came up and turned in his cap.

After everyone had left, Charlie Brown walked slowly off the field.

He didn't go home, however.

He was so discouraged that he sat down on the sidewalk with his
back against Mr. Hennessy's hardware store, and just stared into space.

Suddenly Linus burst out of the store.

"CHARLIE BROWN! GUESS WHAT! Mr. Hennessy wants to sponsor our team in a real league!"

"What in the world are you talking about?"

"Mr. Hennessy wants to be our team sponsor! He said he'll buy us uniforms and equipment and enter us in a real league!"

Charlie Brown couldn't believe his ears.
This was the answer to a life-long dream.
"Wait till the rest of the kids hear this!
OH, BOY! This is just the thing to bring my team together again.
REAL UNIFORMS!"

By this time, of course, the other kids had forgotten all about baseball. In fact, some of them had filled a plastic wading pool with water, and they were splashing around in it having a good time.

"HEY, TEAM! I have the greatest news of all time!" shouted Charlie Brown. "Oh, good grief, Charlie Brown, why don't you leave us alone?" "But listen! Mr. Hennessy is going to buy us all real baseball uniforms! He's going to be our sponsor! We're going to have real uniforms and play in a real league!"

"HOORAY!" they all shouted. "Charlie Brown has finally done it!" "Okay, Charlie Brown, you can count on us. We're still with you."

Charlie Brown ran all the way home.

He had never been so happy in all his life.

For once things were working out right for him.

Just as he got home he heard the telephone ring, and when he answered it, he found himself talking to Mr. Hennessy.

"Gee, Mr. Hennessy, you sure are a nice person. This is the greatest thing that has ever happened to me."

"Girls? Yes, we have some girls on our team.

A dog? Why yes, Snoopy,
my dog, is our shortstop.
He's the best shortstop you've ever seen, Mr. Hennessy.
He what?"

"But, Mr. Hennessy
   . . . but

. . . but,

I don't understand . . .

I see . . .

Yes, I know that
rules are rules . . .
But these are my friends,
Mr. Hennessy, and Snoopy
is my dog . . .
How can I tell them that
this league doesn't allow
girls and dogs to play?

I can't . . .
I just can't.

No, I'd rather give up
the uniforms.
I know it isn't your fault,
Mr. Hennessy . . .
I'm sorry, too . . .
No, that's all right . . .
You did your best.
I appreciate it . . .
Thank you . . .

Thank you for calling.
Goodbye."

Charlie Brown hung up the phone and put his head in his hands.

"I can't stand it. I just can't stand it."

As he went out the front door of his house,
he found Linus coming up the front walk.

"I can tell something is wrong, Charlie Brown. I can tell by the way you look."

"You are a shrewd judge of human nature, Linus."

"Mr. Hennessy just called, and I found out that this new league
our team was supposed to be in doesn't allow girl players or dogs.
How am I going to tell them that?"

"You're doomed, Charlie Brown," said Linus.
"Why don't you do the obvious thing? Leave town!"

To make matters worse,
Charlie Brown discovered that his team
was out practicing,
and without his even telling them.

They were so enthusiastic
about getting real uniforms,

that they were making sensational catches

and hitting the ball

like they had never hit it before.

"Well, I might as well tell them," thought Charlie Brown. "But I'll try to break the news gently."

**"OKAY, GANG, GATHER 'ROUND HERE.
I HAVE AN ANNOUNCEMENT TO MAKE!"**

"C'MON, TEAM! OUR MANAGER IS CALLING US!" cried Lucy. "When this great manager who is responsible for getting us real uniforms calls us, we'd better answer right away."
"You can forget the uniforms," said Charlie Brown. "I told Mr. Hennessy we didn't need them."

He turned and walked away.

For a moment the kids were stunned. Then they rose to their feet and began yelling at Charlie Brown.

"YOU BLOCKHEAD! You never do anything right! What's the matter with you? **YOU STUPID BLOCKHEAD!"**

Charlie Brown didn't stop. He kept right on walking.

Just then Linus spoke up.

He faced the other kids who had been shouting insults at their manager,
and he said,
"YOU OUGHT TO BE ASHAMED OF YOURSELVES!"
He told them the whole story of how Charlie Brown had refused to
take the girls and Snoopy off the team just to get uniforms.
"HE'S SUFFERING MORE ABOUT THIS THAN ANY OF YOU ARE!"
cried Linus.
"Charlie Brown wanted those uniforms more than any of us, but he wouldn't
sacrifice his friends! I'm ashamed of all of you!"

"I KNOW WHAT WE CAN DO," cried Lucy.
"Let's make Charlie Brown a special manager's uniform all of his own!"
"That's ridiculous," said Linus. "You don't know anything about sewing, and you don't even have any material!"

"OH?" said Lucy, and she looked right at Linus's blanket.

They all ran off to work on the uniform with Linus running
along behind, keeping a worried eye on his precious blanket.

You have never seen such activity. Snoopy was in charge
of the tailoring because he knew his master's sleeve length and neck
size. Poor, worried Linus was the one they used as a sewing dummy,
and he suffered terribly as he saw his security blanket rapidly being
turned into a manager's uniform.

AND WHAT A UNIFORM!

Well, when Charlie Brown saw it, he was so happy a big tear rolled down one of his cheeks.

There is nothing that makes a manager happier than knowing he has the loyalty of his players.

A game had been scheduled for the next day, but unfortunately it started raining early in the morning, and it was one of those rains that just sort of settles in and you know it is going to keep on all day or even all week long.

"Only a blockhead would be out on a day like this," said Lucy, as she and Linus stared out the window.

And sure enough.
When Linus put on his raincoat and went out to the ballfield,
there stood Charlie Brown on the pitcher's mound.

He was wondering where everyone else was!

Linus didn't say anything.

He noticed, however, that Charlie Brown was wearing
the new manager's uniform that had been made
from his blanket, so he reached over
with one hand, and took hold of
one shirttail, put the thumb
of his other hand in his mouth . . .

. . . and he and Charlie Brown just stood there in the rain.